M. J. Gorton

The Drama of the Cycle

M. J. Gorton

The Drama of the Cycle

ISBN/EAN: 9783337342555

Printed in Europe, USA, Canada, Australia, Japan

Cover: Foto ©Andreas Hilbeck / pixelio.de

More available books at **www.hansebooks.com**

THE
DRAMA OF THE CYCLE

AND OTHER POEMS

M. J. GORTON

BOSTON

JOSEPH GEORGE CUPPLES

250 Boylston Street

MDCCCXCI

CONTENTS.

PREFACE.

Bishop Butler in the introduction to his Analogy bases his Argument on the doctrine of probability. Voltaire, in an essay on judicial inquiries, teaches, also, that probable evidence is the basis of action in the affairs of life. "Moral action," says Mr. Gladstone, "is conversant almost wholly with probable evidence."

The fact that moral duty may be studied in the light of the progressive spirit of man down through the ages, under the crucial test of scientific scrutiny, does not hinder the fact of statement so conceived and so stated, that, true to the laws of moral evidence from the standpoint taken, the premises and conclusions are just; and yet the result may shock the finer sensibilities and traditional instincts of a differently cultured public. The plea that the dreary code of the morality taught in the "Kreutzer Sonata" is repulsive to western nations, does not affect the fact that the book is moral in fact and in statement.

The Oriental idea that marital love, even when approached and lived in the purest manner, is looked upon as an unclean thing, and this base view of passionate expression, is happily without recognition among western nations.

Music, Sculpture, Art, the Drama and family affection, and that form of Romance which generates into altruistic development, are recognized as the foundation of pure living and clean morals, and encourages the highest expression in Art, and on this view of progress as opposed to that adopted by Count Tolstoi — with the probable evidence of scientific truth in this statement of morals — is the argument on which " The Ballad of the Cycle," is founded and sung.

To condemn all expression of Art save that used in worship of the Highest is to limit the intellectual range and dwarf the affections, but to progress toward the Good, the True, and the Beautiful by advancing from the Seen to the Unseen is the pathway of natural growth.

M. J. G.

IOWA CITY, IOWA, March 10, 1891.

DRAMA OF THE CYCLE.

BEFORE Time was, the Eternal
Lay and brooded in the darkness,
In the vast and silent darkness,
Till a fragment of his Spirit,
Slow-detaching from his substance,
From his substance immaterial,
Forming into misty masses,
Into misty, tremulous vapors,
Slow-evolving in the darkness,
Ever stretching farther, wider,
Lay around the great Eternal,
A huge globe of frothing vapor.
Then the great Omnipresent
Breathed upon this misty vapor
And the currents of his breathing
Set the whole in whirling motion,
Drove the globules of the vapor
Into balls of greater denseness,

And he breathed and blew upon them,
With his breath he formed them
    whirling
Fast and ever faster ; as the
Potter shapes the vessels swiftly
Whirling, so the Great Eternal
Shaped the misty, vapor masses,
Drew the globules close together
Of the vapor, faster whirling,
Formed the sun and all the planets
From this misty, whirling vapor,
Gave them each their place in heaven,
Marked their pathway plain before
    them,
Set the bounds of their outgoing,
Bade them come again in circles,
In vast circles, never meeting,
Ever coming, ever going,
With the rapid whirling motion
That his breathing gave unto them,
When from mist he shap'd and
    form'd them.
Deep in the trough of the whirlwind,
Dashed the hail, crashed the thunder,
Zigzagged the fiery lightnings
Through the gloomy night, yet shape-
    less,
As the darkness closed upon them,
Lay upon these worlds in motion.
Then the mighty One, outstretching

His strong right hand, touched the
    planet
With the touch of his forefinger.
At his touch glared the lightnings,
Flared in mighty conflagration,
Burst the sun in kindling grandeur
Full upon his brother planets,
And his warm light shone upon them
With a warm and radiant blessing.
Straight the power of the Eternal,
Till then slumb'ring in the darkness,
Thunder-rolling took on substance,
Clothed itself in forms of beauty
Round the cliffs and heights of
    mountains,
Flung a mantle of green verdure
Till the Earth was clothed with gar-
    ments
Gay embroidered as for a bridal.

(*Magician of the Dust.*)

    Straggling atoms,
    Solidified being,
    Of precious gems
    Subtler form seeing.

    Flying in mist,
    Filling the river;
    Buried in dust,
    Changing ever.

Another basis,
Hidden from light,
Crimson gashes
Throbbing to sight.

In arctic glacier,
Wrought in lava heat,
Crushed rock masses,
Feeding yellow wheat.

Object-lessons in the Earth life,
Gay 'broider'd as the sun shone on it,
Shone on the Earth green-vested,
And this mighty force, glad-quick'n-
        ing
Greater powers of the Eternal,
That still lay in heavy slumber
That a babe knows ere its waking
To this life of sin and sorrow,
Stirred them up to greater action.
And they took new forms upon them,
Forms of beasts and forms of fishes,
Forms of birds and forms of cattle,
Till the Earth with life was teeming,
Till the primrose and the snowdrop
Gem'd the Earth as the stars the
        heavens,
And the water, clear as crystal,
Showed the gliding forms of fishes.
    And the Spirit, the All-powerful,

Breathed the breath of life through
    nature,
That the air might be health-giving,
That the Earth might bring forth
    plenty;
And the water, rippling, sparkling,
Through the grassland, through the
    woodland,
Giving moisture to the herbage
And pure draughts to thirsty crea-
    tures;
Swiftly onward flowed the rivers,
To the bed of the great ocean,
Filled it full to overflowing,
Peopled it with flashing fishes.
    And the heaving mass of waters,
Caught the motion of their cradle,
Of the Earth, the ever whirling,
Formed the mighty rushing current
That lies warm beneath the tropics,
Rising from the storm-toss'd ocean,
'Neath the belt of the Equator,
Ever flowing, gliding onward,
With a grand, majestic motion.
   Then the warm sun, warmer beam-
    ing
On the breast of the broad ocean,
Drew up clouds of wat'ry vapor,
Raised them till they hung suspended,
High above their parent fountains,

On the breast of their earth mother.

(*Magician of the Mist.*)

Wordless gloom,
Speechless doom,
Was overcome by struggling and rev-
olution;
Conflicts fierce,
Storms and peace,
Were the products of varied evolu-
tion.

Day and night,
Darkness, light,
Passed thro' birth throes, and were
girded, ere the earth
Settled to order
From centre to border,
Or meditation was, or thought had
birth.

Sweet melody,
Exact harmony,
Caught their tone from the humming
spheres ;
Growling thunder,
Lightning's wonder,
Gave forth dread, awe, hatred and
ghastly fears.

As things took form,
Time was born,
Seasons became years, years passed
into epochs ;
Dateless ages,
Bodiless breaths,
Are pall-bearers of Time to Eternity's
crypts.

(*Spirit of Creation.*)

Lying about in the pure ether
Were mighty powers of the Eternal,
Strongest essence of his Spirit.
With the power of multiplying
Taken from the dark Earth's bosom,
With the gift of ceaseless motion
Won from rivers ever-flowing,
With the vasty depths of being
Stolen from the tossing ocean,
With the breath of life eternal
Drawn from winds world encircling,
With the warm and radiant blessing
Of the sunlight shining on them,
These great powers of the Eternal,
Of the Mighty, the All-powerful,
Lay upon the shining vapor
Of the clouds in heaven soaring,
Mused and pondered on the being
Of the green Earth far below them,

Marked the motion and the changing
Of the powers of the Eternal,
Of their mighty lesser brothers
Who took forms of herbs and cattle,
Living on the round Earth's bosom.
    And they saw this ever-changing,
Ever-moving life beneath them
Went by law and not by license,
Went by order, grand, eternal,
In which naught was lost or wasted,
But throughout the ceaseless changes,
Moving in appointed order,
The beginning held the ending,
And the end a new beginning.
    Then these greatest, grandest forces
Of the mighty Father Spirit
Throbbed throughout their mighty
        being
With a thought, grand, all-absorbing,
With a thought of highest grandeur,
And they said, with deep communing:
Down below us there is motion,
And the ceaseless change of forces
Changing into one another,
Following each its law of action,
Moving on in blind obedience
To the great will of the Creator;
We will take their life upon us,
Live among our lesser brothers,

Like them live in ceaseless changes,
Like them follow laws of action,
As demanded by the Great Spirit.

(*Chorus of Spirits.*)

Ere light had birth,
The chrysalis earth
Was the tempest-toss'd scene of
conflicts and death;
The mosaic mind
Of all mankind
Was wrought from chaos, the wind,
storm, breath.

Hopes and fears,
Smiles and tears,
Were of Creation's experimental
trials;
Ere Adam began,
Or ever Eve span,
There were tremulous vibrations of
tears and smiles.

Wisdom and folly,
Sanity and frenzy,
Sprang from the Stygian depths of
storms and strife;
Darkness and light,
Weakness and might,
Strove as mighty giants ere matter
won life.

ᴜ_ i and evil,
Angel and Devil,
Were coexistent from the beginning;
Love and death,
Discord and breath,
Mingled their cries, ere mortal was
born to sinning.

(*Spirit of Creation.*)

Ere mortal was, the spirits saw
All the world-wide, pregnant diff'-
rence
'Twixt the deeds of Good and Evil,
Bound themselves by right laws
only,
Promis'd then obedience conscious
To the laws and rules of action
Of the Great Father, the Eternal.
At the end of the communing,
Of the fruitful consultation,
These high powers of the Great
Spirit
Gently sank down through the ether,
Softly lighted on Earth's bosom,
Took upon them shape and features,
Stood erect most radiant creatures.
Thus man was born, self-conscious,
Knowing well both good and evil;
Partaking of a double nature.
Man and woman formed the Ego,

Double in form, but one in species ;
Thus, two in one, from the beginning,
Heaven born, but earth nurtured.

(*Spirit of Evolution.*)

When Nature had made all her
    throng, —
Plants and beasts (their name is
    legion), —
Gave each its zone, and place among
Created forms of its region,

Look'd she for one nobler, higher,
Commander of this motley host,
With aptitude for life where'er
Life can flourish from coast to coast.

Man came, and he partakes most
Of rhythm, of discord, worse than
    either,
As he guards the helpless lost host,
Or lives for self, regarding neither.

If man, guided by superstition,
Degraded by a human creed,
Human God, damning devil, question
Which is master, both serv'd at need.

(*Spirit of Creation.*)

Hence man, pursuing both good and
    evil,

Sees that man's lesser brothers,
Birds and fishes, plants and cattle,
Follow straightway Nature's teach-
    ings,
For they had no power of choosing,
Knew no law but that of Nature ;
But men had the power of choos-
    ing, —
Ere train'd in ethics, such choice
    made they.

(*Spirit of Man.*)

VANITY.

Old Vanity, head uplifted,
Glances haughtily around,
With self-esteem is gifted,
As he jauntily treads the ground.
Murmuring gayly, as he minces,
A bacchanalian song,
On his head ringèd tresses
Are tossed as he walks along.
Ah me ! how shallow, how silly, is
    life to him whose brain
Is careless of being lov'd; and lives
    his day in vain,
Who ever thinketh of self, brooding
    visions that enchain.

PHILOSOPHY.

A sound of joyous shouting
Upon the air swept by
From the school; Philosophy,
At the Académé, close by,
The master taught the pupils
With tales of the roaring sea,
By changes of the earth and sky,
The fire flaming merrily, —
Four elements to eternity.
" In atoms, the joys of earth," he
    said, " the gods have sent; "
As they blend in one, and life is
    short, let it in joy be spent;
Seeking always pleasure, let gleeful
    song and wine be blent.

LABOR.

Swindling leeches that fatten
On poverty's lean emptiness,
Rolling in silk and satin
And gilded expensiveness,
Finds man a dull machine,
The sum and aim of life,
To live a narrow purpose mean,
Grasping, with greed and strife,
Usury from honest livelihood.
For wealth is hugging self, despite
    hunger and rags,

At cost of Labor's lean stomach and
    moneyless bags;
Forgotten: "As the work so the
    reward is," — best of adages.

SENSUALITY.

Sirens with tinkling voices,
Bright eyes and golden hair,
Drank cups of ruby clâret, —
Enchantment, with visions fair.
And one, the fairest vision
Amidst the shouting crew,
First kissed the ruby goblet
Excess held high to view;
"Come, pledge!" she cried, with ac-
    cents wild, as notes of any child:
"Pledge to me! I to you!" The
    infatuated youth, beguiled,
Drank to the dregs, and awoke, de-
    serted, and went mad.

EARTHLY WISDOM.

Wisdom teaches well this lesson,
"Put not your trust in any man."
We mourn that the restful trust,
Of two-thirds our allotted span,
Should be our faith betrayed,
To perish in the outer cold;
Those who clung to us in summer,
Have gone away as we grow old.

Ah me ! killing, chilling, is the solemn
    trust betrayed ;
Save to yourself the roses, when the
    pale snowdrops fade;
There is no help in any child of man,
    howe'er displayed.

DESPAIR.

Despair, to shun the revel,
And rushing of the throng,
Sought a solitary level,
Far from where men came along ;
But like the merry sportsmen,
That surround their prey,
The eager band press forward,
To bar the poor man's way.
Ho ! wait for us, thou sad one ; wipe
    those weeping eyes of thine ;
There is no help on earth, therefore
    cheer your soul with wine :
But sorrow digged for himself a
    grave, before his faded prime.

(*Spirit of Evolution.*)

Why continue ?   See what sadness,
Man, unrestricted, chooseth ever !
Look ye ! the unknowing brute beasts,
Birds, plants, fishes, all creation,
Taught by instinct, not by reason,
With no learning, no traditions,

With no speech, no way of telling
Wisdom learned to one another,
See, they grow and thrive and
    prosper,
Wrought out works of greatest
    cunning,
Built the comb to hold the honey,
Wove soft nests for tiny birdlings;
Lined with color soft shell-houses,
Lined them with the tints of heaven,
As when the round-orbed sun is
    setting,
Painting them with colors tinted,
As no human hand could paint them.
All these things man's lesser brothers
Did by following Nature's teaching,
Following straight in blind obedience,
All the laws of the Creator,
Laws electrical and eternal.
But their inward conscious knowledge
Puffed men up with pride and envy,
And they straightway left obedience,
Silly grew, as lacking guidance —
Found they broken law compelling,
Something higher than earthly wis-
    dom —
Some exposition to 'scape chastise-
    ment,
Caught by the woes of excess, vanity,

Labor's woes, despair, the irony of
    fading years.

(*Spirit of Progress.*)

Misfortunes, criminality, acts beyond
    control,
    Too late,
Brings agonizing defeat, and the
    result
    Is fate.

(*Spirit of Evolution.*)

If wisdom seek, men may by obedi-
    ence overtake;
Laws, if observed, soften the rulings
    of cruel fate.

(*Spirit of the Ages.*)

From him that hath not, shall be
    torn what he hath;
    Storms rend the living oak,
    Flames follow lightning's stroke;
So might wins Earth's sanction, but
    failure her wrath.

Figs grow not on thistles, nor grapes
    on thorn trees;
    From the bud springs the flower,
    Thus strength begets power,
To cover the land, from seed sown by
    the breeze.

The soul that sins, shall many lives
    overwhelm, —
Stern decree, but ever true !
    For lost is ship and crew,
Though void of offence, if a fool be
    at the helm.

If light shine in darkness, the dark-
    ness is great ;
    To outward form strict,
    Pharisaical, exact,
The inward life perishing, dying
    from hate.

The fathers ate sour grapes, the
    children suffer sore ;
    Not alone does man live,
    His excesses others grieve,
Condemning to pain, by heredity's
    power.

Time weaves the web, wrought of
    joy and of sinning ;
    Purity in one age,
    May become sacrilege,
Culture determines so, since the
    beginning.

But in the shadow the Eternal twists
    the thread ;
    For he understands,
    How frail are human hands,

And that goodness and faith by life-
    blood are fed.

The strongest ever live, the weakest
    must go ;
    Thus Nature has spoken,
    And though hearts be broken,
Deepest love cannot save him who
    is his own foe.

Into the tangled threads, love and
    faith are blending
    Golden gleams of prayer,
    Frightens away despair,
Despair to resignation, send trium-
    phant ending.

Life's living, fate's doom, leads to
    bitter heart-break ;
    But Charity's birth,
    And smiling, brave worth,
Teaches victory may the darkest
    doom overtake.

What a man sows, that alone shall
    be his reaping ;
    Another sows not in my field,
    I garner not his yield,
The fates guard each harvest, while
    man lies sleeping.

(Spirit of Creation.)
Men, not beasts, broke the laws of
    being,
Marked out paths for their own
    liking,
Laid out roads for their sweet
    pleasure,
Setting up their ideal fancies,
For the guide-posts of their pathway,
Murmured that the will of Heaven,
Ruled still in spite of impulse —
For ever above the narrowed view
Of man's selfish vision, a mystic
    rhythm,
In God's own time, keeps truthful
    measure.

(Spirit of the Ages. Cry of the Masses.)

    Greater might for the stronger,
    Less strength for the weaker,
The world has no aid, for the brother
      in need ;
    But gathers to squander,
    Poverty's scant beaker,
And empties the cup, in the hogs-
      heads of greed.

    Royal gifts for the mighty,
    But tax from the lowly,

So riches shall gain more, while
    want shall still lose ;
    And nothing buys slightly,
    Either wicked or holy,
And the poor sell their lives, in pay-
    ing Earth's dues.

    Give aid to the conqueror,
    But strike down the fallen,
Any crime save defeat, a man may
    redeem ;
    For success is the flower,
    And fame is the pollen,
That sets the false fruit of wordly
    esteem.

    Ringing shouts for the victor,
    But scorn for the vanquished,
Though one be a boor, and the other
    a king ;
    For fate recks not how godly,
    The heart that is vanquished,
When wounded and torn by failure's
    dread sting.

(*Altruistic Spirit.*)

Labor groans in throes of travail,
Looking for the strictest justment,
When it brings mediæval vestments,
To the world-market at fixed prices.
Lo ! the fibre now demanded,

Is stuff of wool, linen, silk and cotton,
Machinery made by forces invisible,
Suitable to changeful climates,
Suitable to man's wants, everywhere,
Peopling all the plains and mountains,
Reducing wildernesses to man's
  wishes,
Co-operating for man's needs, in
  living,
Will give to perishing souls their
  share.
'Tis bitter folly gold to offer,
When universal iron is needed,

(*Spirit of the Ages.*)

Or deliver message by Herald's
  trumpet,
When lightning is page to the Stock
  Exchange.

(*Cry of the Metropolitan Masses.*)

In the vile street,
All sins do greet,
And mingle with the hoarse roar of
  crimes effete ;
Wretches beer-sodden,
Laborers down-trodden,
Famish'd, shrink to cold garrets,
  starving children to greet.

Foul, arid homes,
Slime-garbaged stones,
Drenched with squalor, and grey
    with rotted horror;
Vile-visaged tramps,
Under glaring lamps,
Shout curses, and crowd pale helots
    into the gutter furrow.

Living they sicken,
Their doom to quicken,
Gladly closing a life they never
    fully lived;
Fire dying or dead,
The boards a bed,
They die in filth, and rest unknown
    in Potter's field.

(*Spirit of Evolution.*)

Whence comes human development?
For man's progress and enlightening,
Is not bitter biting hunger,
Cold and nakedness the factor?

(*Cry of the Citizen.*)

I must have bread,
For I hear with dread
The mills are closed, there is no work
    where we dwell.
No work can I see,

Earth has no room for me,
Want, ghoul-like, is sucking life,
  until our souls rebel.

  Shall I steal bread ?
  I must be fed :
Work I must have now, or I shall
  go mad.
  " There is plenty of bread " —
  Is that what you said ?
" None to-day ? " — why work, when
  work is ever denied ?

  The felon has meat,
  I starve on the street,
And sleep at night amid snow and
  sleet ;
  What crime can I do,
  To provide a home, too ? —
Prisons, only refuge for the proleta-
  riate.

  (*Evolution Spirit.*)

Civilization, what answer ? —
Innocence appeal, sorrows cry ;
Else bitter hatred, fiercest strife,
Frenzy, despair, wholesale slaughter.
Never changing, never varying,
In the spinning, in the weaving,
In the living, in the dying,
Is progression, retrogression

Onward action, degeneration.

(*Mephistopheles.—Organic progres
sion, against Degeneration.*)

Load the scales, the weights adjust,
The balance is against man, ever,
Let him struggle and strive,
At odds with life, howe'er clever !

Virtuous life, three score and ten,
Comes now a vile temptation ;
Sin-fallen, life-smitten, cursed,
Now to Eternity, by theologian.

Vile action, impure the fountain,
Of those yielding temptation,
Ere death, latest intonation,
Repents, wins ecstatic translation.

Fresh cream for Gods Olympian,
Few sour drops, spoils the potation ;
Mould, — spite of incantation, —
Reverse, sweet to sour, no reaction.

Blackness of doubt, and grim despair,
Nestles amid the orange bloom ;
Life abounding, fervent prayer,
Swooning, droops down into the tomb.

(*Progression.*)

Charity, hopefulness and faith,
Trinity, divinely pledged,

Does lighten the lowliest path,
From infancy to the tomb.
Back into the soft green meadows,
Back into the happy pathways
Trod by those who give obedience,
Knowing, willing, glad obedience
To the will of the Eternal,
Turned the wayward children gently,
Clothed the moral law with vest-
    ments,
Welcoming mystical Religion
Interpreting death in Resurrection.

(*Mephistopheles.*)

Pleasure on earth, beauty in heaven,
Springs from passion well-directed ;
Soul unto soul harmonized, self
Held in check, the dross extracted.

Shock electric passes, hits man,
Sets him brooding, strikes out self ;
Love, the awakener, grips him, —
Jealousy transforms to demon-elf.

(*Evolution.*)

Passion seems the primal fountain
Of music, sculpture, work artistic ;
But the passions, if unbridled,
Lead to sorrow and oppression.

When Mercury led
　A pure maiden free, —
On her shining head,
　The wreath of mystery, —

Through the bright south
　They onward sped ;
He kissed her mouth,
　Rosy and red.

Love wove his chain
　Of deepest gold ;
Worn in sun and rain,
　The tale grew old.

His soul grew weary
　Of the hated tie ;
On a morning dreary
　He saw her die.

Rueful, he fled
　Where none pursue ;
Visions of the maid
　Her memory renew.

Thoughts of the slain
　Follow the youth ;
He left the plain
　Where perished truth.

To mountain heights
　Then fled the youth, —

The mountain of Dry-facts, —
When he had slain Truth.

Lost, love and youth,
But visions still
Remind the Epicurean
That Nemesis can kill.

When passion is out-breaking,
Trespasses with unlicensed will,
The Spirit of Humanity
Decides the " Thou-shalt-not " and
" Thou-shall."
Deep the moral fibres striking,
Ruling still the wild rebellion,
Led these lost and erring children
Through the depths of wild morasses,
Through deep bogs of evil-doing,
Through much of sorrow, much of
striving,
To value the worth of virtue, —
Virtue tempted, virtue yielding,
'Gainst virtue tempted, never yield-
ing, —
To the fountain-head of virtue,
The All-powerful, the Eternal.
And they daily grew in knowledge,
Learned the worth of truth and jus-
tice,
Till one day there burst upon them
The grand lesson of forgiveness,

And the wondrous gift of loving ;
Not the loving of one's household,
Not the love of home and children,
But grand love, wide-embracing
Every being, good and erring,
That mankind counts in its numbers :
Each living for the good of others.

ALTRUISTIC.

(*Youth Singing.*)

Oh, Paradise, where art thou !
  Amid frost, amid flowers,
Amid roses, amid snow, —
  Is it found amid summer hours ?
I have sought thee my life long,
  Night after night, and day by day,
With prayers, tears, and with song,
  All the long tedious by-way.

(*Progress.*)

This is the way to Paradise,
  No gold can purchase your way,
But love in maiden's eyes,
  And love can show love the way.

(*Maiden Singing.*)

Oh, I found a four-leaf clover,
  And I put it in my shoe,
And I wished a wish upon it,
  For they say it will come true.

Chorus — Oh my lucky four-leaf
    clover,
  Lying hid within my shoe,
Bring the wish that I am wishing,
  Or my heart will break in two.

What I wish I must not whisper,
  Lest the charm should be undone;
But I have a bashful lover,
  And he is the favored one.
    Chorus.

But I know full well he loves me,
  Though he ne'er a word has said;
For he trembles when he sees me,
  And his face turns white and red.
    Chorus.

But he is by far too bashful,
  To suspect he's won my heart;
Though, if smiles could give him
    courage,
  I'm sure I've done my part.
    Chorus.

If he should now come a-wooing,
  I will surely tell to you
What I wished upon the clover,
  That I hid within my shoe.
    Chorus.

And for fear he grows no bolder,
   And my wish should ne'er come
     true,
I will tell him of the clover,
   That I hid within my shoe.
    Chorus.

(*Lover.*)
Oh, love is the Paradise
   Of the wandering pilgrim;
Home is the shrine and prize,
   This side of happy heaven.
Wisdom, silver, golden wealth,
   Glory, learning and fame,
Far in just value beneath
   Wedded love and bliss, great name.
(*Spirit of Evolution.*)
Many ages, many lessons,
Were required to give this teaching,
*Adulterous else — from this bind-
    ing
Comes terms endearing, sister, broth-
    er,
Husband, wife, children, father,
    mother,
Confederation sublime.
   Man is now slowly conning,
Dimly, darkly comprehending,

* This thought Browning develops with great
beauty.

All the worth, all the importance,
Of these lessons, of these bindings,
To solve the onward, upward rising
Of the human spirit, tending
Ever to a broader, grander outlook,
To virtue, justice and unself,
To truth and divine forgiveness.
  Do you ask why this working
Of the Power of the Great Spirit,
Down through the race for all ages ?
Why this forming of the planets,
Why this birth of plant and creature,
Why the form of man appearing,
And to what the whole is tending ?
Poets answer all the wherefore,
All the reasons that are asked them.
Life lives not, except in motion ;
Life is motion, death is quiet, —
Nay, is but another motion,
Is a backward retrogression,
Till life, seizing firm upon it,
Fills it with deep-glowing vigor,
Builds it up in other structures,
Other forms of plant or creature.
Hence the Great One, the Eternal,
By his very law of being,
Felt the need of growth and motion,
Knew that there was life in action,
For he would not meanly perish,
Since he is, and always will be.

SONG OF THE FAIRIES.

(*Spirit of Creation.*)

When new souls come down to our
    earth,
  The fairies are busy as busy can
    be,
Making ready, with laughter and
    mirth,
  The statue for the thought hither-
    to free.
      One flies to the west,
      One flies to the east,
      At Love's behest,
      Singing cheerily, cheerily.
High up in the sky, on a sunny day,
  There floats soft clouds of fleecy
    mist;
There is where unborn spirits stray,
  And gently float, as the spirit list.
      Loving thoughts around them,
      All the day through;
      Loving care surround them:
      This is what the fairies do.
They gather sweet honey from the
    bee-hives,
  And nectar from clover and col-
    umbine tips,
And mould it and mix it, as if for
    their lives,

Then add fresh sweetness from vi-
olet lips.
> Whether shady or sunny,
> Their work they pursue,
> So loving and bonny :
> This is what the fairies do.

At last the statue takes the infant's
form :
They wrap it in rose-leaves, soft and
white,
And tinge the lips with carnation
warm,
And underneath the eyelids slip the
light.
> Eyes from the blue sky,
> Hair from thistle down,
> Life from lightning flash,
> Breathing and warm.

(*Evolution.*)

Caught life from the Great One, the
All-powerful :
He, moving, felt life glowing in him,
And he knew that he was living,
By such laws and rules of action,
Born within his mighty bosom
(Creation follows law, not license,
Else the world would be chaotic).
Thus was formed all the vast system,
From the substance of His being,

From his being, electrical.
　When the pathway of Creation
Has been trodden to its ending,
There the place of the beginning,
Also, lies in the vast circle.
In this universe of wonder,
With its wealth of sun and planets,
With the broad earth, fruitful, bear-
　　ing
Plant and creature, and Earth's chil-
　　dren,
Latest born and fairest favored,
Men, the wise, the law-abiding,
All will join this mighty being.
Man, the foolish, the law-breaker,
May gather the Sodom-fruit of Chaos;
But justice, in the courts of heaven,
Will hold the balance and will gather.
All who have the force for being
One, uniting with the Parent,
Will become again a portion
Of the Mighty One, All-powerful,
Who will take their new being,
Form new worlds by constant motion,
Far above the comprehension
Of mankind, the question-askers.

THE ABODE OF MATERIA PRIMA.

YLIASTRON.

'Mid Zarrahs of space are new
    thoughts born,
To take on dream-shape as night
    sweeps by ?
Through the dim silence they go and
    come,
And in the darkness recede to die ?

Trembles the faint gleam of thoughts
    unsung,
That creep and creep amid human
    tears,
Of those who lacked strength to live
    and sing,
And died unheard in the bygone
    years ?

Or do souls inhabit the dim night
    wraiths ?
Those who once knew triumph and
    heart-break,
And now know sleep and bodiless
    breaths,
Whose forgotten thoughts arise and
    awake.

From thence come new ideals, start-
    ling change,
Fashion'd by inventors, who strive
    'mid scoffing,
Seeking for earth's hidden force, the
    mainspring
Of Time's birth, on far Eternity's of-
    fing ?

Or the wordless gloom of a song un-
    sung,
That lay buried in the clay-bound
    soul;
The strong earth-bands loosed, it
    floats along,
A rhythmic harmony, a rounded
    whole ?

Or the moaning, or the faint sad cry,
Of those who pant amidst want and
    scorn,
Bowing and dooming in fevered la-
    bor,
The myriad lives yet unborn ?

Or the phantasmal glow of the soul's
    light,
Ever springing through the magic
    night,
Struggling to know dawn, and to win
    sight

Of the latent source of strength and
    might ?

Or the despairing cry of the Spirit
Of those who would vocalize unknown
    strands ;
Those poor mortals who find not such
    merit,
Till Death lead them to quiet far-off
    lands.

THE UNDER SIDE OF THE WEB.

So long as busy Time shall feed
    Her web, of many colors dyed,
Self-sacrifice and selfish greed
    Run through the pattern side by
    side.

The rocks were powdered long ago,
    By glacial cold and lava heat,
Ere vine could climb or water flow,
    Or fertile earth yield yellow wheat.

Men bless the tender wayside spring,
    But if it fail, from lack of rain,
Their angry voices loudly ring,
    The while its scanty cup they drain.

The tender, clinging, ivy vine
   Lends sturdy oak an airy grace,
But as its tendrils closer twine,
   The tree is doomed by its embrace.

It ever was since Time had birth,
   And thus will be till Time be dead;
No good has ever blessed the earth,
   But what it was by life-blood fed.

A MORTAL'S DOOM.

There was beauty in the summer
   skies,
   Or hopelessness of black despair;
Hope sung to joy in sweet surprise,
   Or days were full of sorrow and
   care.
      Sorrow and care,
      Joy and sorrow,
      Is ever your fare,
      Upon each morrow.

Dreamily, solemnly, to and fro,
   Wearily crooning a rhythmic song,
A mystic shape, moving ever slow,
   Kept pace with me as I went
   along.

It was my doom,
The hidden fare,
On to the tomb,
Of joy or despair.

I gazed into the dim mirror's face,
    Where, I was told, faintly shone
The future's surest, truest trace
    Of that rocket's track, a mortal's
        doom.
            A picture true,
            Of future life;
            Honey or rue,
            Joy or strife.

In that dim glass odd fancies run,
    And take on shape in the silent
        gloom;
Through the lone watches they go
        and come, —
    A soul faltering on the verge of
        doom.
            But this is truth, —
            The soul's doom ever, —
            As ye sow in youth,
            So age must gather.

Time told the truth, Fate was rul'd by
        me,
    And I held in my fingers the
        thread

Of what I am, shall do, and what
    shall be, -
  I make life a thing of joy or of
    dread.
      If good prevail,
      Joy is the end;
      What men call fate,
      Is life turned friend.

ON FRIENDSHIP.

**SUGGESTED BY A ROUMANIAN
PROVERB.**

Thou mayest gaze on cloudless skies,
  When summer winds are bringing
Earth's sweetest perfume from the
    fields
  Where busy scythes are ringing;

Thou mayest see a perfect rose,
  By cottage door-cheek growing;
Thou mayest find a flawless pearl,
  With purest lustre glowing;

Thou mayest woo a peerless face,
  Of beauty most bewitching;
Thou mayest win a loyal heart,
  Thine own with love enriching;

Thou mayest feel the sweet heart-
    throb
That thrills a lover's greeting ;
Thou mayest know the heavenly
    bliss
Of fond lips slowly meeting ;

Of perfect things thou mayest find,
    The list indeed is endless ;
But never search for faultless friend,
    Lest thou for aye be friendless.

WHIP-POOR-WILL.

Loud rang the voice of the whip-
    poor-will,
    Singing to the poppy so red ;
The heart of the poppy, a-thrill,
    Sank as it were dying or dead.
        " Love, O love, my love ! " he
            cried,
        " Open thy fringed eyes to me ;
        " Thou art ever my queen, "
            he said,
        " Why droopest thou so wea-
            rily ? "
Still sang the voice of whip-poor-will,
    All night so mournfully it fell ;

Faithfully its soft, plaintive call,
　Beseeching love for whip-poor-will.
　　　"So sadly thou droopest" he
　　　　said,
　　　"So lowly bows thy lovely
　　　　head,
　　　O love, my love! poppy so red,
　　　Come, come, my queen, low is
　　　　my bed."

Slowly the poppy unfolded
　Her fringed petals to the rain ;
But her hue, from a ruby red,
　Faded so white and so wan.
　　　The raindrop saved the bride ;
　　　But alas! her heart was chill.
　　　Lonely and true at her side,
　　　Sang the faithful whip-poor-
　　　　will.

LESSONS IN LIFE.

Time lack I for empty seeming,
Wish lack I for idle dreaming ;
From sun to sun firm facts are mine,
Teaching life's lesson line by line.

Duty done by self and neighbor,
Living earned by honest labor,

Cares and trials and pricking thorn
Met with brow like a summer's
 morn ;

Kind words spoken, loving deeds
 done,
Hatred and malice held toward none,
Trust in God, and faith that his law
Maketh the mighty sun to draw

From the sea's broad breast the drop
 of rain,
To water, on meadow, field or plain,
Some tiny roadside flower that
 grows
Where no man plants, but God himself sows ;

Trust that the God who careth for
 this,
Will keep his child from going
 amiss :
These things make a triumph,
 though one
Of no man honored, by no man
 sung.

Though poor and plain my life seem
 to thee,
Yet these things make a triumph
 for me ;

Heart's fullest joy and content are
    mine, —
I learn life's lesson line by line.

SONG OF LIFE.

Life is action, life is motion,
Rising, falling, like the ocean ;
Moons are fulling, moons are wan-
    ing,
Naught at stand-still is remaining ;
Suns are rising, suns are setting,
Men are losing, men are getting ;
    Want and plenty rank are grow-
      ing,
    Sow your choice, and reap your
      sowing.

Life is doing, life is working,
None gains aught by idle shirking ;
Hours well spent in honest labor,
Brings harvest, to self and neighbor.
Thistles tall will fields encumber,
If ye lie in idle slumber ;
    'Tis the weeds unfit for reaping,
    Sow themselves, while men are
      sleeping.

LAMENT OF THE GUERILLA'S WIFE.

AN ARKANSAS BORDER BALLAD.

Th' track at th' turnin',
You er' discernin',
Is where I us'ter look an' look fer
my man,
When, his day's work dun,
At th' set o' th' sun,
He'd kum wi' sum game fer me i' his
han'.

Now, orn'ry th' evenin',
I set heyr a-grievin',
And set, an' set, an' sob heyr by my
lone;
I set heyr a-dreamin',
By th' fire a-gleamin',
A-listenin' for his step on th' door-
stone.

Eh! but love is sorrer,
Too bitter t' borrer
Fergettin' as th' shadder kums up th'
hill;

Th' crick as it flows,
Tribbles o' my woes,
An' I git inter th' deeper shadder
    still.

At our weddin' solem,
I tuk me er colum,
An' I stud him onter it amongst men
    thet hi';
He wuz my idol,
Up on a ped'stal,
An' I kep' him thar wi' a hankercher
    on my eye.

My man, he deceiv'd me, —
Would death had bereav'd me,
Afore my mate had condescended so
    low.
Thet we must now part,
Thet breaks my heart;
But yit — we're married till death:
    thet was my vow.

Eh! my joy an' pride, —
Would I had died,
When I wuz sech a desprut happy
    creetur.
It do me sech good,
Ter reck'leckt how proud
We two wuz: hit beats all human na-
    tur.

We wer thet pore,
Th' wolf wuz at th' door,
Thet winter long an' col', an' no work
    at all;
Bread thar wuz nun,
Nor ary stray bone,
Times wuz thet hard.   Well, my man
    had a call

Ter go ter th' West,
Ter make er ter bust.
He lef' me his las' red, when he sed
    farwell, —
Wuz off like er shot.
Dear suz! came a blot
On his fair name; but I clings ter
    him still.

Futher will he roam,
While I bide alone,
Sence his las' desprut chances o' mis-
    doin';
An' I mus' keep on,
To do right by my lone,
Seein' I kin keep us by weavin', 'um-
    bledoin'.

So I set by the gleamin',
Lone harth, a-dreamin',
A-wishin' an' a-wishin' fer thet time
    so old,

When he was so near,
When he was so dear,
Thet all ither love seems common
    and cold.

When Jim comes agin, —
Fer I look fer him,
Day an' night, night an' day, an' all
    the year thro', —
I will claim him,
I will name him;
Tho' no ither would speak ter him;
    I'll be true.

THE BRIDGE.

Casually, my idle wandering
    Brought me to the river side,
Where the bridge, with curving
    arches,
    Spans the swiftly flowing tide;
And listening to the murmur
    Of the waves against the pier,
While the music of the water
    Sung a song unto my ear.

From the bridge so far above us,—
    Sang the waves in silvery tones,—

Come the notes of joyous laughter;
 Come the sounds of sighs and
  moans;

Come the bursts of smothered weep-
  ing
 That betoken bitter grief,
Till the swiftly falling tear-drops
 Bring the sad hearts some relief.

Now a maiden weeps her lover,
 Who her face has soon forgot;
While a drunkard's wife, low sob-
  bing,
 Speaks loudly of a sadder lot.

Or a street waif's tears are welling,
 Because he lacks a father's name;
While a father's slow, salt tear-drops,
 Fall fast for a son's deep shame.

All these tears come down unto us,—
 Sang the waves in sadder notes,—
And we bear them swiftly onward,
 As we bear the laden boats.

But with us they must not mingle
 Lest the stream with death should
  flow,
For these drops of purest crystal
 Are poisoned with human woe.

But the warm power of the sunshine
  Draws them upward in a mist,
And they wait at Heaven's gateway
  Till time shall have ground its
    grist

Then these bitter, burning tear-
    drops
  Shall be changed to draughts of
    gall,
And each must drink from that chal-
    ice
  Who once caused those tears to
    fall.

REST AND PEACE.

I sat on the jutting headland
  And gazed down o'er the plain,
While o'er low hills to westward
  Waved silvery veils of rain.
Snow-white, in towering masses,
  Swift on, the storm-cloud drew,
Till misty, rain-shot curtains
  Hid plain and farm from view.
The storm passed by with its wail-
    ing,
  The sun sank down to rest,

The eastward-stretching shadows
  Lay dark on fields storm-prest.
My heart grew free from its brooding
  O'er long-borne grief and pain,—
And rest greeteth us as surely
  As night the wind-swept plain.

REMINISCENCE.

Forget the past, 'tis full of pain!
  Friendship says, with kind intent:
Others may forget, but I
  Could easier from myself be rent.
The past has made me what I am,
  And in its bosom bears the shape
Of what I will be, as the vine
    Brings forth the flower and then
    the grape.
What if the past brought pain! Ah
    well!
  There never was a grief but taught
Grand lessons joy could hardly tell,
  And views of life with knowledge
    fraught.
My friends, the past I'll ne'er forget,
  But from its days two ros'ries
    make:

The one to help me bear in mind
   Sweet truths I learned by sad
   heartache ;
The other, strung from happy hours,
   Full rounded in their bliss, I'll lay
Above my heart, and tell it o'er,
   To cheer me when life's skies are
   gray.

And in these ros'ries, richly worth
   The pains they cost, kind friends,
   I'll keep
Life greatest treasures, truth and joy,
   Till life for me shall fall asleep.

SOUL LIFE.

Give your soul some time for living,
   Refresh your life with joyous
   mirth,
And win a taste of Heaven's pleasure,
   'Mid the endless tasks of earth.

Who will ask when you are fading,
   What you did in such a time ;
Yet hours spent in needful resting
   Will give time for thoughts
   sublime.

Friends, by-and-by, will cherish
  Words of counsel you may say,
Much more than your weary working,
  When your life is passed away.

There are other hours coming,
  Take, then, some joy in this;
Half an hour less spent in toiling,
  To-morrow's tasks will never miss.

A BALLAD OF MAIDEN LANE.

IOWA CITY, IOWA.

Can't I kum in ? —
I'm so glad I kin;
Fer I kum erlong afeerd an' by my
    lone.
W'y, then, did I kum ? —
Kase I got no home;
And my bar' feet tech th' hard o' th'
    cold stone.

So nipped they are,
An' bealin' an' sore;
An' nobody ever wishes ter see my
    face.
Back er Close's mill,

I hide thar still ;
I's no chance wi' th' odder kids as
    has a place.

I cries by my lone,
But no good kin come,
When yer little, an' lone, an' so
    hungry an' pore.
    Arter yer gits grown,
    Misshun folks kum,
Tend ter yore soul, — can't hear little
    kids any more.

Ther' is sich er many,
If yer tend to any ;
They would find there's sich er
    many forlorn,
    Who has no fader,
    Nor yet a mudder,
An' they was never ast 'erbout wher'
    they was born.

I heerd kerreck,
An' I reck'leck',
The misshun man sed, " Chilrun's
    angels at God's door."
    But Lord ! is that so ?
    When we cries to you,
An' we're allus so mis'ble, an'
    hungry, an' pore.

I jist did kum,
Kase me see one
O' th' kids comin', an' she did say
thet nice,
" Th' teacher'll be glad
Ter see a pore kid,"
An' I want'd ter see one who'd like
ter see my face.

THE HOUSEWIFE'S ROUND-
ELAY.

Tired am I of plodding duties,
Tired of life's dull daily round,
Tired of the prosy tread-mill,
Tired of tasks that do abound,
Tired of my narrow pathway,
Tired of the bare dark ground,
Tired of *being*, doing nothing,
Perforce a modern martyr crowned.

Oft I've listened to the story
Of the heroes of our earth,
Of the toilsome rugged pathway
Leading to the throne of worth.
Michael Angelo, a scullion,
Proved his soul of heavenly birth;

Sketched wondrous visions fadeless,
 With the charcoal from the hearth.

Christine Nillson, though a peasant,
 Taught herself the way to sing
From the birds among the treetops,
 Till like them her voice could ring.
Great Giotto was a sheep-herd, — ˙
 Sketched his flock in yielding sand;
Struggled upward to be foremost
 Of the world's great artist band.

Robert Burns, though a ploughman,
 And while toiling in the field,
Wrote his poems, telling simply
 What his world to him revealed;
And his lines show to what purpose
 The common things of life can
  yield,
When the pathos is unfolded,
 Which in all life lies concealed.

Then upon this sunny morning
 There is no time to weakly cry,
While the bonny sky is smiling
 And there is time and health to try.
There is joy in simple living,
 Doing all that can be done;
Reaping joy, because joy giving,
 Receive the price of merit won.

BARGAINS.

"All the world's a stage
And men and women are but players."
That's wrongly said. The world's a
    mart,
Where all is valued, bought and sold,
By strictest measure, truest weight,
And naught brings simply naught, no
    more,
No less, and none may pay a price
Too high or low for what he gets.
Thou bringest thither so much vice
Or so much virtue, so much done
For good or evil, and receiv'st
From justest scales the fullest worth
Thy treasure merits. If thy goods
Doth please thee not, then blame the
    price
Thou gav'st, not the things that thou
Hast purchased: they are fully worth
All that thou didst pay for them.
    Perchance
Thy offering was scant in weight,—
And, though it were thine all, it ne'er
Could gain for thee thy heart's desire;

And though thou bring'st even more
Than is demanded, still thou'lt fail,
If thou should'st offer gold when iron
Is wanted. True in weight and right
In kind must be the price thou
    bring'st,
That it may gain thee what thou
    want'st ;
Yet e'en the worst of bargains yields
A wealth of value far beyond
Its cost when viewed aright, although
Thine eyesight, blinded by desire
For other things, may see it not.

There weeps the mother o'er the
    babe
For whom she gladly would have
    died
That it might live. She hath done
    much
That most is worth the doing, yet
O'erlooked the foul drain's poisoned
    breath,
And all her deeds of good can ne'er
Restore the child she lost through
    lack
Of doing one most needful thing;
And yet it well may be that could
Yon mother see the path that lay
Before her darling's feet in life's

Wide field, her tears would cease
To flow, and she would ne'er regret
Her darling's future in the upper fold.

Omnipotence
Sees clearly, and when the wage of
    woe
Is paid, that by sloth is justly earned,
Or by ignorance, with open hand
Is compensation given, and our ills
Are overruled to become blessings
From weary pitfalls.

But, best of all,
Yon mother from the woe may learn,
That when the earth enfolds unto
Her bosom and takes into her arms
Her sorrowing children, — when, far
    from
The present bitter blight and cold,
Our babes are taken, evermore to live
In fairer valleys beyond the tide, —
'Tis not life's saddest sorrow,
Although we cry, and, unreconciled,
Blame Zeus, who claimed his own.
But to be life and soul bound as one,
Sharing love's light and gladness; all
Inspiration in communing, each with
    other,
Springing from the glad presence
Of one to that baptismal other;

That change may come and build
Between these sacramental sealed
    units
An everlasting wall, —
This is the saddest thing in life to
    me .
The saddest thing in all the world,
To the disunited, lone, sad souls,
That once were a contented whole.
Faith can teach yon mother, in her
    woe,
That life is one of the leadings given
To teach trust in immortality;
And having humbly bowed her head
Before the will of God, may now
Regain her babe, —no wall between
Her and her tenderly loved.
And she can feel it near her till
Her own weary feet shall pass the
    gates
Of immortality, where is peace,
And tears and partings are unknown.

THE PHŒNIX.

AN ALLEGORY.

There is many a seed that is wasted,
  There is many a birdling dies,

There is many a bud that withers,
  There is many a heart that sighs ;

But seeds there are in plenty,
  There are more young birds in the
      nest,
Fresh flowers are ever springing,
  And hearts that ache love best.

The life that has seen no sorrow,
  The joy that has felt no pain,
The love that has known no heart-
    ache,
    Grows   parched   like   the   sun-
      scorched plain ;

Salt tears may give way to laughter,
  Deep griefs laid aside for new joy,
Sorrows add fresh sweets to loving,
  Pleasure alone is apt to alloy.

The wasted seed brings a harvest,
  Summer songsters sing as before,
New buds on bruised plants are fairest,
  The heart again with love runs o'er.

Learn to drink of death and of life,
  To take of grief and of pleasure ;
Learn that naught can live or die
    lonely,
    And sorrow clasps joy as his treas-
      ure.

LITTLE HOMES.

Bare the hedges, droops the clover,
The dancing leaf whirleth down,
The cold is creeping, creeping over,
The green earth groweth bare and
    brown.
  Oh, singing, singing, singing,
    Are the cicalas, are the crickets;
  Oh, endless, endless, endless,
    Are the concerts in the thickets.

Short the daytime, long the night,
And the birds are farther going;
Cold is coming, — cold and quiet,
Gone the time of summer's sowing.
  Oh, the flying, flying, flying,
    Of the birds strong in flight,
  From the land in twilight lying,
    To the land of warmth and light.

Oh, the lonely, lonely, lonely,
  Little homes in trees o'erhead;
Oh, the lowly, lowly, lowly,
  Little homes beneath my tread.

Summer is dying, autumn is flying,
Low hangs the red sun in the
west;
Winter is coming, snow is trying
To close the doors of homes at
rest.

Wild the storm-blast, — wilder grow-
ing, —
The crickets, singing, gather inside;
Chirp, chirp, chirp, — ever chirping,—
Little homes by the warm fireside.
Thickets shield the brave snow-
bunting,
Eerily, cheerily, in the snow;
Little homes have not Baby-
bunting, —
Little homes are closed by
snow.

THE VERDICT.

AN ARKANSAS BORDER BALLAD.

Ye say ye've kum to lynch the chap
That shot Jedge Brown? Then I'm
The man yer lookin' fer; but drap
Yer gun down, pard. Go fine!

I holped to hol' a lynchin' bee
    On Roarin' River in the May
Ov '73. The man wuz free
    Ter tell hiz side hiz way.

As he tol' hiz, kin I tell mine ?
    I kin ? All right ! Who here
Remembers Charlie Coast ? Well, I'm
    What's lef' o' him ; that's clear.

Ye'd not know les' I tol my name,
    Fer twenty years hez lef' a mark
On my old phiz. Besides, I'm lame ;
    Fell into a shaft in the dark.

'Hurry up? Talk fast ? ' Kerrect !
    I left
A wife and child behin',
When I skipped out. Kate made the
    heft
Ov our hard livin' alone.

She'd had the chice 'twixt me and
    Brown,
    An' picked on me ; I wuz
Good-lookin' them days. All the
    town
Watched us git spliced. Dear suz !

It duz good 'ter reck'leckt thet day,
    In spite of all thet's cum

And gone sence then. 'Shet up?'
  Now, say!
Jest wait till I git done.

Ten min'ts ain't much ter giv a man
  Thet's gwine ter swing. I sed
Kate merried me; Brown had the
    san'
Ter say if she was dead

It'd be better lots for her. We
  Wuz pore; times wuz hard,
You bet! It cut me deep ter see
  Kate at the wash-tub, pard.

When I'd no work I lef,' ter make
  Er bust in Joplin. Luck
Went clean agin me, an' th' break
  I made, one night, ter buck

Th' faro-bank, tuk my last red.
  Nex' day I writ a line
Ter tell Kate I wuz wus nor dead,
  But hoped sh'd still think kin'

Ov me. "She'll marry Brown,"
    I thought;
  I didn't know what luv
A woman haz. It can't be bought
  Nor beat, nor will it shove

A man out-doors if he is mean
  An orn'ry: Kate sed "No"

Ter Brown. But when at last he seen
  What she sed had ter go,

He turned 'ter Bell, our child;
  Talked sweet, give her a ring,
Then lef' her with her good name
    siled, —
  Jest as sum man may bring

Yer darters down ter shame. Poor
    Kate
  Knelt ter him, and pray'd he'd
    right
Th' gal afore it got too late;
  His teeth show'd like they'd bite.

"I begged yer onc't," he sed, "and
    now
  I'll giv yer back agin
What you giv me, — a no." I 'low
  He made the devil grin

An' angels cry. Kate went away,
  Ter hide from her ole fren's,
And watcht our fourteen-ye'r Bell
    die;
  Then sent fer me. Two fiends

Got after Brown, — the devil and me.
  I did my work; I shot him:
The devil hez got his to do,
  Red-het, bilin' over, now he's got
    him.

Men's no noshun what a mother feels
  Beside a grave like thet;
Hit givs a wound that never heals,
  But allus burns red-het.

Well, Kate's dead now; died las'
    week,
  And lies side o' Bell.   I see
Her thin, white face, an' hear her
    speak,
  Rite now.   There's wuss for me

Than hell in livin', — hurry up!
  I'm glad Brown's dun fer; I 'low
He'll do no more devil's work.   Tut!
  Kum on, now!   What's th' row?

I kin go, kin I, scot free?   I —
  I know yer fair ter me, pard;
Thank yer.   But I would sooner die;
  To live alone and damn'd is hard.

LIFE AND DEATH.

From the under-world up to warm
    sunlight,
I struggling pressed, and passed
    grim Death,

A gaunt shadow shrinking from the
    sight;
His misty scarf enwrapped me, his
    breath
Struck chill and cold: "Thou art
    mine," he saith.

Death, — Life, — so much to each,
    day by day,
Careless I, striving on to heights
    imperial;
A mist-like form confronted my
    pathway,
Grim, spoiled, distorted, material:
"Life as thou hast lived it," — false,
    unreal.

So this is life! Memory's sad snatches
Of fiery conflict, pain, blind hope,
    combine
With sunny bits and jubilant catches,
To point the arrows along this
    route of mine:
'O life! hard and bare is thy decline.'

Naked and stripped, thou art grim,
    O life!
Death pursues with grasp of mailed
    steel;
But memory and hope renew the
    strife,

And join the note of life : I feel
Beyond Death's grim margin lies
    the real.

THE CHOICE.

Why piece from out the dry dead
    leaves
Of long-past days a prickly dress,
Thick-lined with mem'ries that will
    sting,
    Though joy come close with soft
    caress ?

Were it not wiser far to tread
    The bruised flax beneath thy feet,
And with its softest fibres weave
    A new white robe, so bright and
    sweet ?

Still all the glory of the clouds,
    And all the fragrance of the flowers,
Shall gather around thy every step,
    To brighten e'en thy saddest hours.

The choice is thine ; 'tis thine to
    choose,
    'Twixt robe of joy or garb of pain.

Choose well; the dress once surely worn,
    Needs must, through all of life retain.
Live, then, thy life!—in each to-morrow,
    Bury the pain of the yesterday;
Let hope spring from the grave of sorrow,
    And gather joy on thy onward way.

HOME LIGHT THE BEST.

I've wandered through the forest
    Where sunbeams dance and quiver,
I've spent long hours a-boating
    By moonlight on the river;

I've risen ere the dawning
    And climbed the mountains hoary,
And watched the sun awaking
    To flood the world with glory;

I've lingered in the twilight
    To view the sunset fading,
I've gazed into a dewdrop
    To catch the rainbow's shading;

I've looked on all lights earthly
  And know which beams the
    clearest,
It is the glow of firelight
  On hearth and faces dearest.

HIDDEN SORROW.

Is there canker in the rosebud?
  None can tell that this is so,
For the evil deep is hidden,
  But the rose will never blow.

Has the tree been struck by lightning,
  Time may heal the wounded part;
But the tempest fells the oak-tree,
  For 'tis wasted at the heart.

Thus may pain and sadness wearing,
  Through a whole life send its taint;
Though the lip should ne'er cease
    smiling,
  Lest it utter some complaint.

Wordless thoughts oft tell the trouble
  To the hearts whose love is best,
And there's grief that thou art griev-
    ing, —
  Sadder grow they at thy jest.

Turn, sad one, turn from sorrow;
  Forget that the earth is sad;
For none can scatter gladness,
  If the inner heart be not glad.

For this is truth the poet sings,
  Choose the robe thou would'st re-
    tain;
For the mem'ry of vanished things,
  Is thyself, be it joy or be it pain.

NORA'S LOVE.

"Love me, Nora, my darling;
Love me, once and again;
Oh, tell me that you trust me,
And I'll be the truest of men."
  The laughing echo, down in the
    glen,
  Mocked back gaily—"truest of
    men."

"My mother says, 'Be careful,
When words of love are spoken,
For if men go a-wooing
Their vows are lightly broken.'"
  Soft sighing echoes, like a token
  By angels sent, sobbed — "lightly
    broken."

"Your mother's heart is jealous,
But she has loved and mated;
She cannot keep you always,
Our meeting has been fated."
    And, like a story twice related,
    The words re-echoed — "has been
      fated."

He threw his arms around her, —
The moon was shining clearly;
"Dear one, your eyes are speaking, —
They say you love me dearly."
    The lying echo murmured merely;
    Earnestly whispered — "love me
      dearly."

Clingingly she trusted him, —
True always and a day;
He left her to long vigils, —
"I will not be long away."
    The low echo laughed, that sad day,
    Mockingly, saying — "not be long
      away."

Long afterward with loving words
She greeted him, at their home
Where, truth and falsehood wedded,
Falsehood said, "I never will roam."
    The bantering echo, light as foam
    Blue waves carry, said — "never
      will roam."

The world was in love with her,
But he broke her heart day by day;
" Good-by, Nora, my sweet darling,
I will not be long away."
   The echo spoke truth, that baleful
     day,
   When repeating the words — " be
     long away."

She cried, " Why has he left me?
Must I bear our shame alone?
No tears have I for weeping,
And my heart is turned to stone."
   The echo low answered, making
     moan,
   Like a lost soul wailing — "turned
     to stone."

The world heaped scorn upon her,
Who had given love and trust;
But honored her false lover,
Wearing robes of crime and lust.
   The ages echo the cry — " Is it
     just,
   That faith must suffer for giving
     trust ? "

THE SONG OF THE SEA.

On that morn the waves sung a cra-
    dle song,
  As they lovingly kissed the warm
    sand,
Where Oona stood watching the fish-
    ing smack,
  Gaily sailing away from the land.
    Oh! the sea has songs it loves to
      sing,
      In the ear of the fisherman's
      wife,
    As she watches the boats, and
      prays for them,
    And the loved ones far dearer
    than life.

At the set of sun loud wailed the sea,
  And it sang of the harm it had
    done,
While Oona stood gazing away wea-
    rily,
  For the boat that held husband
    and son.
    Oh! the sea has songs, etc.

The storm passed on, the sea softly
    moaned
A dirge for the boat on the reef,
And Oona in wordless pain lay on
    the ground,
    While the stars looked in on her
    grief.
       Oh! the sea has songs, etc.

Still the sea sings on, its sweet cra-
    dle song,
    And the men come safely with
    their catch;
But to Oona there is ever an appalling
    note,
    For no son now lifts the latch.
       Oh! the sea has songs, etc.

THE RAINDROP.

Rhythmic murmurs amid the rainfall,
    Followed the rounding of the gem,
As the drop fell to the heart of the
    snowball,
    Like a pearl from Spring's diadem.
    Chill, chill, O snowball,
       Moaned the raindrop in its
       gloom;

Thy heart, O snowball, is chill,
  And pale in its breathless
  doom.

There came a breathing at night-fall,
  That stirred the drop in its grief;
Sinking downward, the raindrop
  Fell to the innermost leaf.
    Chill, chill, O snowdrop,
      Cried the raindrop from its
      tomb;
    Thy heart, O snowball, is chill,
      And pale in its breathless
      gloom.

Dark and deep the raindrop lay cold,
  Entomb'd since its fall in the
  show'r,
Until the mist drew upward, extol'd,
  This gem from the heart of the
  flower.
    Again it fell as a dewdrop,
      Burning and bright, its heart
      afire,
    Flashing its flame from the pop-
      py's cup, —
    This was the flower of its mad
    desire.

THE LONE SLEEPER OF
THE LOS ANIMAS.

On a slope, rock-sown,
Of a gulch alone
'Mid the spurs of the Los Animas
    mountains,
Where a rippling brook
Glides by a quiet nook,
On the way from its snow-fed foun-
    tains;

There a sobbing pine
Sings, in slowest time,
'Mongst the scattered and wind-
    swept grasses,
Over a narrow mound
Of pebble-strewn ground,
Scarcely to be seen through the cac-
    tus masses.

A rough board of spruce,
For monumental use,
And a rose of Nature's wild planting;
Broken stones in disorder,
For the wall's low border,
Toward the still, lone sleeper are
    slanting.

Sparkling with early dew,
Crocus-cups of dainty blue,
With the earliest spring are blowing;
Purple asters nod,
Beside the golden-rod, —
'Neath the summer's warm sun are
glowing.

But no woman's love
Tends that lonely grave,
And no grief mars that lad's calm
sleeping;
A mother's heart lies
Beneath that rise,
Where the spruce-tree its watch is
keeping.

For a ruined cabin,
And a shaft caved in,
'Mid the rocks with lichens hoary,
Of bootless quest,
And endless rest,
Sadly tell the pitiful story.

THE PHILOSOPHERS' MIS-
TAKE.

Much they talk of law and order,
   Of the rule of each on earth,
Tell us of the deeds of nature,
   But they fail to explain birth.

They show us all the wondrous work-
         ings
   Of our frames in taking breath,
But their very wisest wisdom
   Cannot save that frame from death.

They prate learnedly of living,
   Say this world is full of strife,
And the fittest wins survival,
   Yet they know not what is life.

All their learning is the knowledge
   That force acts by certain laws,
And they show its way of working,
   But they cannot tell the cause.

Their mistake is not in saying
   That law rules us by its rod,
But in preaching "laws of nature,"
   When they should teach "laws of
        God."

BALLAD OF LIFE ON THE UP-GRADE.

With candle dimly burning
    In the night,
In Earth's deep heart, yearning,
    I toiled with might.
'Neath porph'ry, rosy red,
Veins of rich ore-beds led;
Masses cunningly enclosed
    In crystal star
    Of sparkling spar.

Low-roofed was the narrow drift,
    With heavy girders;
Pungent fumes of powder lift,
    'Mid heavy vapors.
There we toiled for eight long hours,
Stifling save at apertures
Of narrow shafts, breathing doors
    For the new morn,
    From Heaven let down.

Into the bucket gladly springing
    To mount aloft,
I slowly rose, twisting, turning;
    Then stood abaft

The throbbing engine, where the chill
Of the fresh-born air of the hill
Pulsed in my being, athrill.
      Upon the stroke
      My mates awoke.

The first faint morning breeze
      Stirred without,
Sending a shiver through the trees
      Standing about.
'Neath a dead tree's limbs was seen
The full-orb'd, round-disc'd moon,
With dim aureole, presaging doom
      Of coming storm
      Ere another morn.

Towering peaks touch'd heaven, east-
      ward,
      Grandly gleaming ;
Outlin'd, each crested mountain, west-
      ward,
      Thread edge, a silver lining ;
Smoky clouds in furrows weltering,
These grand heights snug sheltering
The vale of Bois d'arc, checkering
      The landscape wild
      O'er mount and field.

Fields tilled, yellow stubble,
      Joined the foot-hills ;
Slowly rising, the slopes double

Into billowy swells ;
Torn, as the raging torrents dashed,
The full-rounded folds were washed,
And ripp'd by gulches gashed,
   As the fierce fountains
   Lash'd the nude mountains.

Aspen, oak, pine, quaint cucumber
   Fringed Bois d'arc,
Heavy growths of pine and cedar
   Crowned Ozark ;
Uprear'd its high peaks i' the dawn-
   ing,
Round its forehead played the morn-
   ing,
Crimson glory purloining
   From rosy fingers
   As the sun-god lingers.

Darker swells, 'twixt glowing catches
   Pink and salmon,
Changed and deepen'd to brighter
   snatches
   Of flaming crimson ;
Then fleecy grew, like surf breaking ;
Then golden gleamed, partaking
Of victory. Sun-god, awaking,
   The cloud-veil rent,
   Gracious splendor aslant.

Stretching forth a glittering arm,
   He clasps aside,

In his embrace so ardent, warm,
    His earth-bride;
Awaking birds begin to chirp,
Cheery sparrows flitting, flirt,
Thieving crows, jays, saucy, pert,
    From bough to tree,
    Twittering softly.

The birds astir, gave life to Nature —
    Peaceful strife!
The engine pulsing made small stir,
    And noisy life:
Master of all, man, the miner, —
Coarse in thought, all the finer
Life crushed by hardest labor, —
    Living, corpse-fashion,
    Soul cramped in.

Slowly leaving the shaft shop,
    At the summit
Comes to view a fearful blot,
    Where the sunlit
Path extended down the slope;
Fruitage pensile from a rope,
Red-ripe, unplucked, — no hope
    Of toothsome bit
    From facet-flash fruit.

Came a sudden woman shriek,
    Dwarfed all else;
Sympathy flashes, as a spark,

Each human pulse.
Rush of men, faces a-pinch;
Ha! more work for Judge Lynch!
Given an ell, they take an inch, —
Regulators!
Investigators!

Thick fog-curtains, swiftly rising,
Veiled the sun;
All the glories comprising
The golden ocean
Of floating clouds departing,
The scar'd birds hush their chirping;
Flakes of snow fell, softly whirling,
As a cover
To disorder.

To look upon the livid face,
Dilated eyes,
Flawless mask, — of life no trace, —
Hellish prize!
Who heard the agonizing groan,
The fruitless prayer, the maddening
moan,
The struggle in the dark alone?
In bitter gloom
Meet such a doom!

On a spur of the Ozark's,
'Mid pebble-strewn ground,
O'er looking the valley of Bois d'arc,

Is a narrow mound, —
A slanting stone to mark the spot.
His history was ne'er forgot;
His memory kept clean from blot,
    By woman's breath
    And woman's faith.

A maiden sings above his grave,
    This little song,
Commemorating her brave,
    To right her wrong.
For she knew not the true tale told:
Her lover died for love of gold, —
For love of it, his soul he sold, —
    A murderer
    And train robber.

(*Maiden Sings.*)

I'll sing you a song,
    When life to me was gay;
For life is long,
    The skies sad and gray.

Our grief shall last,
    Forever and a day;
Our pleasures cast,
    One gleam and away.

That thou sayest,
    Bears back once more,

The happy days again,
  That all too soon were o'er,

Then I'll sing me of joy,
  Forgetting my grief;
And, in others' gladness,
  My heart shall find relief.

Nay; hear'st that gay song, —
  It brings back once more
That one hour of heaven,
  That all too soon was o'er.

Oh! the sad awaking,
  Again I live it through;
I tasted sweet honey,
  But drank my cup of rue.

The pansy glad may bloom,
  And bud and bloom again;
But hearts are not like pansies,
  Joy blooms but once for men.

And if their leaves reopen,
  The blight is in the flower;
Memory dims its petals,
  Sorrow is its dower.

The ghosts of joys long buried
  Have risen from the tomb,
And all of life's bright sunshine
  For me is changed to gloom.

Too soon I learned the lesson
  Life gives us all to read,
That joy is but the wrapping
  And sorrow is the seed.

(*The Miner.*)

Thus life went: and I, by miner's
      might, —
  Busy on the Up-grade, —
In narrow drift, by flaring lamplight,
  Toiled with pick and spade.
For a mess of pottage, sold my
      heaven, —
Song of birds, shapes in clouds,
      driven
By the sweet air of the even, —
  While I burrow
  In saddest sorrow.

Not as the maiden sorrows, sorrow
      Comes to me ;
But that each sad to-morrow
      Leaves me less free
To see each sunrise — my birth-
    right —
Bursting into glory on the glad sight.
Through the cloud-rifts, bright sun-
   light,
    Buried I must toil
    For wealth in the soil.

If fate would yet grant to me
      Love for yon maiden,
Soon would her sorrow forgotten be,
      By cheer o'erladen.
I'll toil for her, she shall love me,
The light of day shall look on and see;
Love's law straightens inequality,
      That Fate has made,
      In the struggle Up-grade.

(*The Miner's Wife.*)

My life is in a minor key,
      Although I'm young;
Woe and gall have a harmony,
      Demanding song.
The gay hours of youth time fills
With many quavers and glad trills;
The joyousness of Nature thrills,
      Swelling fullness urge —
      Low moans the dirge.

Love's love; loving is the life
      Of woman, —
I should be happy as a wife,
      Being human.
Caresses bring a dart of pain, —
I love my miner, but am fain
Remember buried ghosts, that reign
      In my heart,
      Of the past a part.

While he, my poet miner, mines,
    The day long,
I drink bitter dregs of life's wines,
    And sing my saddest song.
I chant of my fallen idol,
That I mounted on a pedestal,
Which by its own weight fell,
    Dragged to doom,
    And the tomb.

Lost to the world's just esteem,
    How the memory
Cuts, burns and stings, and my dream
    Renews the misery!
So deep in my heart of hearts,
The last sad drama upstarts;
And through each moment darts
    The maddening sight, —
    My life's blight.

Oh, my pride, my joy, who mad'st me
Proud'st, glad'st of women,
How could'st thou sin so wofully! —
    A thing alien
To my love and faith, that were bond
Enough to hold thee, I so truly fond;
And thou didst strike me to the
    ground,
    I unknowing
    To thy vile doing.

And didst thou, my fallen love,
    So wofully suffer ?
Where were thy friends, hand in glove
    With the robber ?
I, alone, alas ! am left to protect
Thy memory, lost to all respect,
Not mentioned by the circumspect.
      Alas ! what a cheat
      Is love like that.

Cold and dismal is my life,
    Worse than alone ;
Since I am an honored wife,
    With heart of stone.
May God send strength, to benumb,
All thought, remembrances that come,
Of him who lies unhonored,
      Of love, not worth,
      Guilty to death.

      Thou chosest wrong,
      I must keep on
Where truth and right do lead me ;
Alone, scorned, another must need be
My all in all, nor yet forbid me
      The memory, bitter-sweet,
      Of thee, Escheat !

      I live again
      That dismal morn ;

I see thy brow, with dismal shade
    creeping;
I hear the murmur, some secret keep-
    ing;
I guessed the wherefore, afterward,
    not heeding
      The stabbing word,
      "Robbed the Road."

      Turn me — turning
      From saddest yearning —
To welcome my noble poet-miner;
Him, — dross extracted, all the finer
Manhood cherished, — almoner
      Of my sad life
      When drugged in grief.

      Long shining shafts
      Through cloud-rifts,
Glancing through the mountain
    passes,
Out of a sky of gold and crimson
    masses,
Wrap him, as he comes, in tresses
      Of fretted light —
      A welcome sight!

      He knows my grief,
      I lighten his life,

By gladness at his daily coming.
Like weary dove, flying to its homing,
His soul straight comes, intoning
Thoughts grand and sad,
Wrought in lives Up-grade.

LES MISERABLES.

The sun shines for us, around us are
built,
We respectables,
Unseen walls to keep us from souls
dark in guilt —
Les Miserables.

O wretched lives! O lost hearts! pin-
ing to soon die,
Why perish?
Asking for bread, charity gives a
stone, hoping thereby
Some good to cherish.

In your foul-smelling homes ye cry
for aid in vain:
"Increase our wage;
Long days spent in toil for bread, life
liv'd in pain,
We die at early age.

" Popular Aid Societies care not for
 human cause,
  But work for self,
To gain the frayed edges of vain self-
 applause,
  Or bit of pelf."

Poor, doom'd lives ! none may change
 the soul within ;
  Yourselves do show
Lack of earnest thought, pure air,
 cleanly living, to win
  From your woe.

Your cry is for wealth, striving for
 golden treasures, —
  Will this cure sin ?
Drive away filth and rottenness at
 the core,
  That stifles the soul within ?

Life must be filled with thought, that
 subtler sense,
  For delight,
That lives, works, breathes pure air,
 thro' new lens
  Wins sight.

Respectability must toil themselves
 to save
  All ; but help they cannot,

Lost souls who are healed not from
    within,
  To better their lot.

CHRISTMAS IN POVERTY ROW.

" Kum erlong, kum, get a move !
    Goin' ter th' p'lice, that's shore;
Santy-Claus, my bloomin' cove,
    Haint givin' picters to th' pore.

"Oh, he brung it right ter yer !
    Kum now, yer small pertaties
Ter hev swell-lookin' picters
    Kum to yer from Santy-Claus.

"I say, wher did yer git it,
    Kid ?   We're no sich blame softies !
How did yer kum onter it ?
    Wher was yer ole Santy-Claus ?

"Yer cribbed it, yer know yer did,
    Outen th' tonies swag;
Yer ketch'd, my bloomin' cove,
    Tryin' to swell, and ter brag.

"This picter is Santy hisself,
    A-skootin' ahin' his nifty deers ;
Wouldn't de kids giv' derself
    A picnic if he'd look a-here's.

"Say, kid, guv me de picter
    Yer must or I'll call th' p'lice.
Then, 'Where did yer git onter
    It?' dey'll ask ye mity fierce."

"An angel brung it, so she did;
    It's mine, kum down from th' windy,
A-swingin' by a teeny thread,
    From the Amen chap'l, ther' Chris-
    mus shindy.

"Ther's my angel now. She's kum,
    Ter fetch kids sumfin what's pore;
Looks like a angel spilt plum
    Outen the sky, that's shore."

"Why, Mabel, this young loafer
    Has your Parian marble statue!
Police! Not a word, Mab, in his
    favor.
Here, take this tramp in charge. The
    rascal!"

Christmas eve! Glad crowds aglee!
Joyous greetings throughout the
    town.
Christmas splendor! Christ's re-
    nown! —
Amid tramps and ruffians unclean,
Christ's child, Scabbie, wept, unfed,
    unseen.

THE MOTHER'S LAMENT.

Col' an' dark,
Stiff an' stark,
Lies my girl i' th' bed whar we laid
her last,
Scorchin', gallin',
Tears are fallin',
Like rain swift and fierce and fallin'
es fast.

Hid from sight,
Lonely o' night,
Is her bed, an' she can't speak, see,
nor stir ;
Worry an' care
Is still my share,
An' she no longer here, an' I can't
come to her.

I'd know her,
I'd follow her,
Oh, my empty arms ! an' oh, my
heart is sore !
Ever and alway,
Day arter day
And night arter night, I miss her
more an' more.

When happy days
Is in our lives,
Thar's a mighty diff'rence 'twixt rich
an' pore ;
When death so close, .
Strikes like a force,
Hit brings together what joy rives
apart so far.

'Tis rich an' high
Mourns with I,
As worship'd the trac' o' her little
footsteps light,
As her trippin' feet
Made prints i' th' street,
As straight and slender as a ray o'
sunlight.

When come noon-day,
They took her from me,
An' laid her by her lone on the barren
hill ;
Like a cold stone,
My heart sunk down,
The sky grew dark, an' life fer me
stood still.

My lone girl-babe !
My purty child !
My one blossom, my pride, my glad
desire !

My tears unshed,
Burned i' my head,
I made no moan and my sight shone
    like fire.

Till one as is rich
Shed tears which
Loosed the dried-up fountains o' my
    tears.
An' when he cried,
"Would she had not died;
Though dead she is my own an' I am
    hers!"—

When love so true,
Comes close to you,
It draws your heart, an' your own
    grief is still.
I walk th' path,
In patient faith,
To the lowly grave upon th' lonely
    hill.

FLOWER AND FRUIT.

Drunk on the wine
Of spring sunshine,
The orchard blossoms free;
Helped by the power
Of summer shower,
The fruit sets on the tree.

With color won
From August sun,
Apples glowing yellow,
At hint of frost,
From boughs wind-toss'd,
Drop down ripe and yellow.

Buds for blooming,
Months for growing,
These bring harvest pleasures;
Blighted flowers,
Stormy hours,
Ruin Autumn's treasures.

In youth's bright May,
Spread blossoms gay,
And manhood sets the fruit;
But old age shows
What apple grows
From spring-time's budded fruit.

THE UNDYING QUESTION.

I agreed one day to act on the stage
  (For my life work, and harvest sow-
    ing),
And in gay mood tried to teach my
  age
  (The law of love, joy, and Romance
  roving).

As I stood on the shore of Life's great
  sea
  (Playing at life's dreams and
  agonies),
I scorn'd the old myths, men-made
  mysteries
  (And felt joy, and taught life's
  ecstasies).

Atoms ever changing, but life en-
  dures
  (Love's law, love's love, ever reign-
    ing),
Life in cycles, motions, endless
  powers
  (Enjoy the hour, the hour its joy
  retaining).

One law reigns and rules over all,
  (The trees and flowers have like
  emotions),

Man and the teeming land in thrall
  (To pleasure's law, and love's
    potions).

Nor Christ nor Pilate was, Ideals
    each
  (Of altruistic rise and ebb),
The fruitful earth glad kinship teach
  (Life is *living*, joyfully, tears all
    shed).

When lo ! from my side to dimmest
    gloom
  (Death stole my one love to silence
    away).
Where is God? To love, is *Joy's*
    doom
  (Law's logic explains not death or
    the tomb.)

Far to the northward shadows are
    slowly creeping,
Burnishing broad realms, beneath
    wide horizons,
Where are few pampered lordlings
    in palaces,
And in mud-huts the sad-eyed fella-
    heens ;
Where are palm-trees and reeds of
    papyrus,
Lotos and crocodiles basking in the
    sun,
And hawk, heron, stork, cooing dove
    and ibis :
A land teeming with a wide, full-fed
    plenty ;
The twilight land, grey, with memo-
    ries haunted,
Of a limitless past backward reaching
    to the dawn;
A thrifty land, with arteries and
    sinews fed
From the life-giving ichor stored in
    icy fields,
Where giant spires shoot straight to
    their crowning,

From frozen gulfs lying betwixt the
    pinnacles,
Above the mists, 'neath southern stars,
    snow-cap'd.
In these far-away mountains, above
    the zephyrs,
Or song of brooding bird or chirp of
    summer insect,
Beside the very grave of life, where
    death comes not,
For lack of life in the frozen desola-
    tion, —
Resurrection far below, in torrent,
    forcing a passage,
Leaps into the Libyan desert, sweep-
    ing, surging,
Groping thro' the mournful sandy
    silences
(Brimming river swelled too, by mid-
    sea freshets,
Rolls on 'neath other stars, far to
    southward),
Down to the land of the Sphinx,
    allegorical witness
Of Time's changelessness in bewilder-
    ing epochs —
So born, so has been, so is, the mystic
    life-giving Nile.

(*Voice of the Nile.*)

Come worship at my shrine,
    Ye sons of toil !
From the desert and the sea,
    I made this soil :
Built the deltas, comprehending
The land of Egypt ; befriending
By eons of toil, work unending.

Pray you, pray ! If I abide,
    There is corn for reaping ;
Let me leave, turn aside,
    Barrenness and weeping :
Stifling sands exterminate
All moving things animate, —
Silence, waste, exanimate.

Far-off, flitting memories
    From a dim past ;
Struggling, grim phantoms
    Of the Won and Lost :
Creatures who liv'd and fed
Upon my banks, then vanish'd,
And others came to fill the void.

Cities sprang into being, —
    City of the Greek and Cairo,
Full of life and living,
    Memphis, Sais, Dendara ;
Spread her wings pillar'd Karnak.

And gnomon Pyramids, gigantic,
Perched on the spurs of Mount
    Mokat.

  Pallid man, the sad-eyed,
    Master-mind, the sculptor,
  Wrought works allied
    To those of the Creator:
Marble! porphyry! Gold! Color-
    ing!
Mighty temples adorning;
Revelry fantastic, towering.

  I have thankless wrought
    For hordes of Earth's denizens,
  And never yet sought
    Nor found remuneration
Of Man: he, of created things,
Is ever plunged in endless war;
I, the unwilling spectator.

  Man, the miserable,
    Even when conqueror,
  Struggles continual
    For balance of power;
Eastern Asia, Western Europe,
Seeking for a wider scope;
Death-grip here, without hope.

  "See, forty centuries
    You to look down upon,

Frenchmen ! soldiers !"
Shouted Napoleon.
Pyramids, by my brim, years —
Uncounted in blood, in tears —
Preceded Tel-el-Kebirs.

'Tis the old, old story,
   Written in stone ;
Nature-worship hoary,
   'Gainst civilization.
If martyr'd shades look down,
In the slowly coming dawn,
Does he the riddle read ?—Gordon !

Struggle as ever 'twixt factions,
   Time is shrivell'd to a jot,
The lists, Egypt's land, to settle
      questions,
   Which is master, which is not.
Inner life, outward action,
Progress tends, of the fraction,
Thrust down, no resurrection.

But I fail not : deepest snow
   Feeds never-failing fountains,
Far-off, 'neath the Equator,
   Gathered on the mountains.
I change not, for I ever feed
This ingrate land at its need, —
Ages and ages as they breed.

Let them pray ! If I abide,
  There is corn for reaping ;
If I leave or turn aside,
  Languishment and weeping.
For I give the palms, corn, lotus,
I feed the cattle, doves and ibis,
All things that are most precious."

The worth of life may be drawn from
  Earth's heart ;
Yet brave as is the show of worth,
  most worthless
Without the murmuring, unpausing,
  ever gliding
Evenly, sinuously fruitful flood slow-
  ly rising :
Thus all are fed by the same unvary-
  ing law, —
Men, beasts, vegetation, all things
  animate,—
And each lives by the law of its
  organic being
Liv'd, fed and liv'd again by law of
  reproduction ;
All but man the insatiable, man the
  greedy.
He, of strength and power of cunning
  cumulation,
Enslaved his brothers, doomed them
  to toilsome labor,

Built Pyramids, huge columned tem-
    ples, palaces,
Statuary of godlike proportions, and
    by speech
And many curious hieroglyphics
    taught the ages
Of his doings, — the toiling millions
    in mud hovels,
The pampered lordlings in their fine
    palaces, —
Also of many devasting bloody battles
In which men strove as beasts, and
    struggling, died.
Slaying, ravaging, burning; yet time
    for yearnings
Fill'd the suffering souls, whose ask-
    ings are not fantasy.

    (*Wailing of a Captive.*)
God dwells in meanest things,
  In ghosts of Ra and Tum,
In beetles, lizards, toads and bugs.
    If murmurs reach beyond the tomb,
      He will hear the shivering sigh
      That friendless woman knows,
      Too proud and pure to sell her
        soul,
    When driven to sin or die.

  We exist, nor can we help it,
    Prisoners to the victor braves,

Stolen from the spurs of Mokat,
  Bound and sold for slaves.
    Oh, happy the people who can
      die !
    For sad the life of all women;
    Sadder yet, if a gentle human,
    Doomed against her will to
      live a lie.

Why dwells not God in woman?
  Why has she not a soul, and a
    place
Among created things, though
    human ?
    Does not the bull receive wor-
      ship, Apis ?
    Be she alive or be she dead,
    Who takes thought or note ?
    Slaves or worse than the brute;
    The seed-bed only, where is
      planted seed.

O God of heaven ! To thee we cry !
  If that thou mads't divine Osiris,
He that rules in fairest sky,
    Mads't thou not the gentle Isis ?
    Within this narrow dreary pen,
    Looking upon a noisome court,
    We fainting die, of men the
      sport,

We too are children of the
dawn.

Men sin, too, if we are slaves
To passion's falsest action ;
They make us suffer to our graves,
Tho' always two form that pac-
tion.
Why man dictate of weal and
woe ?
When two sin, why one sin-
less ?
When two act, why one stain-
less ?
Why yet a *man*, she a *seraglio* ?

(*Old Princess — buying slaves.*)
(*Phœnicia.*) — How   wildly   sings
yon maiden ;
Bring her here, make room.
She looks an Egyptian,
Sings she of her home ?

(*Captive, running, kneels.*)
O Lady !   Buy me, buy !
Protect me from danger.
I will toil night and day ;
Save the poor stranger.

Make me your meanest slave,
I will toil from sun to sun ;

I will bake, prune, weave,
To please your every whim.

(*Princess.*)
Too pretty to bake and brew,
   To fine to toil afield,
What can I do with you,
   Poor, pretty, lost child ?

(*Captive.*)
Oh, let me be your slave ;
   Think of my fate, alas !
With none to pity or to save :
   I, born maid to Isis.

Brought forth of sorrow,
   Bred from my native ooze,
Upon each sad to-morrow,
   My youth and beauty lose.

(*Princess.*)
Veil yourself, your price is paid,
   Follow where my eunuch leads,
Thy name is now Rhodope,
   Rose of the Nile, Rhodopis.

As of eld, the sun rose on the sacred
   river, and shone on Egypt's land,
"Striking, with his first rays, music
   from Memnon's statue on the Nile,"

When the captive maid, now queen
　　of the West, noblest of women,
Return'd to her battle-strewn land,
　　missionary, queen, Savior.

Behind the snowy peaks the day was
　　　　breaking;
　　　Through mists was seen,
　　　Nitocris, the queen,
Advance where light and shadow
　　　gay fretwork making
　　　To her realm,
　　　Land Egyptian.

Shining shafts of light through aisles
　　　　and passes —
　　　In grandeur solemn,
　　　The palm-tree columns,
Lay in gold, crimson, pink and am-
　　　ber masses,
　　　On the floods
　　　Of Nile outspread.

Wrapped by the mist in a wedding-
　　　gown of white,
　　　Sweet mignonette,
　　　Roses with dawn-dew wet,
Cling in fragrance to her shining
　　　garments of light,
　　　Truth her guerdon,
　　　Queen of Wisdom.

Through slavery, pain and sorrow, to
    her place of ease,
    Had this woman,
    Divinely human,
Won her way through formalisms to
    truth and peace,
    By right of worth,
    Fairest Queen of Earth.

(*Song of the Queen.*)
O my people, hearken! Would ye
    reap again,
Mind the sheaves ye bring are of
    golden grain,
For ye must sow aright, if so ye
    would obtain.

At the judgment bar of Osiris, must
    ye all come.
If the life be beastly, comes the final
    knell of doom;
If good, righteousness and mercy
    follow to the tomb.

If ye would be mighty and grow a
    nation strong,
Ye must not bind the souls of any,
    to drive to wrong;
For your women are slaves bound
    with brand and thong.

Ye suffer thereby.   Give them honest
    love and thought;
For Love is pure when shared by
    each, not bought.
The West is right, the East burdened
    with a sadder lot.

That woman's love is brutal, her kiss
    an act of sin,
When lavished on her husband, and
    true to the soul within, —
Here ye are at fault, O my people!
    are slaves to begin.

Slaves are ye born, in bondage the
    mother's groan ;
Your land ever a battle-ground, Civil-
    ization
Will struggle to drive ye back in all
    the years to come.

Grapes grow not on bramble bushes,
    nor figs on the thorn,
All people are growing either thistles
    or the corn,
Sybarites are sowing mighty tares,
    thinking not of the morn.

At morn there is seeking for the seed
    that is sown,

Tears and sorrow follow storing the
    crop that is grown,
Nor think of the sowing — each soul
    reaps its own.

The fruitful sun shines on the just,
    the unjust as well,
But the seed sown in the valley, the
    seed sown on hill,
Must produce of its kind, crop of
    wisdom or of hell.

The Rose of Egypt sung and died in
    Nitocris, Queen ;
Love is daily slaughtered, her land
    still lacks civilization.

THE END.